SEA AND HUMAN

GOLU KUMAR

Contents

DCLARATIONThe purpose of this book is not to hurt anyone's sentiment, this book is written from the heart.

ONE

THE IMPORTANCE OF THE SEA IN PEOPLE'S LIVES

. The only absolute great power on earth is the sea. From the womb of the sea was born the land that is still in insular fragmentation only here and there the all-encompassing ocean interrupts. Only the sea forms between the atmosphere and the Rock armor of the earth as a whole, and the main thing is the earth is still a planet surrounded by the ocean. Also the mysterious origin of organic life we will consider a momentous occurrence within the sea tide of that time think since there was no country and one undivided Ocean surrounded the globe as a concentric hollow sphere-like itself enclosing the atmosphere. But it is the further development of earthly life that takes place uniformly, even those originating land-dwelling plant and animal forms up to the human marine Procedure. Through eons of adaptation to the conditions of existence outside of the Meanwhile, a deep chasm has developed between the creatures of the sea that live on land and sea. True, rivers and lakes, through their Aquatic nature of the sea elective elements of the country, blur in In exceptional cases, the otherwise strictly observed limit of the oceanic fauna kingdom; some fish are outright like eels and salmon Double residents in salt and fresh water, other saltwater fish get used to it gradually to the less salty waters of the estuaries until their Descendants swimming up the stream veins, finally for the duration remain in freshwater, like the small club polyp in recent times Time only from the North Sea through the brackish water of the Elbe estuary in the Elbe and Saale, even as far as the Süßen See near Eisleben. whales give birth on land, powerful fish predators, such as the frigate bird, which Albatross use their mighty wings to fly over the high ground for days Lake thousands of miles from shore. Nevertheless stays the coastline the most thoroughgoing dividing line in the distribution of living beings on earth. And man, his whole organization indicates that his tertiary ancestors were fruit-eating Being a forest inmate was a matter of course from the start exclusive country dweller. The coastal ring of the eastern fortress may be used as a far-reaching outer wall of the home of primitive mankind. The sea can upon man, when he first beheld it, only acted as a deterrent with his in hospitality, with the sudden dangers by which it is the nourishing topsoil of the Mainland threatened in the form of high breaking surf, overflowing floods, terrible storm weather. the far superior he saw himself facing the enemy pressing against him with elemental force defenseless person first pushed into the defensive position, especially since on flat coasts, where the rise and fall of sea levels at high tide and low tide creates tidal currents that reach far across the lowland coast sweep along. Pliny has given us a dramatic picture of this in primeval times warning battle with the ocean from the German North Sea shore handed down, like this to the Roman Empire of the shielding dyke construction was still lacking. Every day, reports Pliny, the Tide stream this land of the Germanic Chauken underwater that the Residents, fled to their huts, resembled seafarers, until then the Ebb current set in and the people like shipwrecked out of their narrow Dwellings lured to fish from the receding sea water catch or glean ejected sea peat from the damp mudflats. Here we can already see the struggle for existence between man and the sea perfected tools guided; the Chauken had already met on self-listed hills, on "Warten", solid building ground created for their huts, as the Hallig people still do today small marshland islands off Schleswig that are therefore not dyked west coast use those. All that was needed was the "golden circlet" of the Dike walls to be pulled along the coast to the amphibious Belt of the interplay of the tides as rich in pasture and wheat to constantly gain heavy marching ground from the German mainland. The man knows from history how many blessings this triumph is ours and has enlisted the Dutch coast dwellers ever since the frieze proud after the last groundbreaking in firm barriers rejected "bare Hans" i.e. shouted the word of victory to the sea: "Trutz now, blank Hans!" and it could be called: ~Deus mare, Batavus litora fecit.~ The score over the otherwise all-powerful opponent Success stiffened the freedom-proud neck and the more incessant that Dike construction demanded joint work for its further maintenance, as it could only be founded through active, self-denying Collaboration of many, the more tenacious unfolded behind this one Fortress wall against the tyrant Okeanos the selfish individual will subduing honorable community spirit, which all State order carries behind it, much like it did thousands of years ago the dam and canal constructions on the lower Huangho, in Babylonia or on the Egyptian Nile. Much more important, however, appears that decisive step which man did in distant antiquity when he feared conquering the unknown, boldly facing the hostile element itself entrusted to navigate the surging sea stretching endlessly before him on a rickety raft, in the hollowed-out log or the raw Wooden timbered boat. More than once like our sex, by extended migrations split long ago into varied hordes, which did not know each other when they reached the shore of the sea, this one has made important progress, the germ of the dominance of man over the earth. where rivers flowed into the sea, could one attempt to reach the high seas in riverboats, elsewhere the impulse produced itself, on the ridge of the sea it continued to move as merely swimming, directly those afterward so marvelously sophisticated art of construction as well as of mariner leadership Vehicles by which man, alone among all creatures, which Boundaries of the shoreline on all sides and to the furthest distances was able to breakthrough. But what on earth drove him to the daring oceanic Risk? Often the hunger, this dark, all-powerful one Educators of humanity, like us, those who search for fish in the ebb foreshadowing spying Chauken; often also likes the escape from one superior enemy tribe in agony made inventive, around the treacherous sea as a temporary refuge from the safe end preferable. But then a tribe took up residence for the Staying on the seashore, two things made it more gradual To educate familiarity with the initially feared element: the Treasure of coastal sea of exploitable sea creatures and waving opposite coasts or both together. The lack of food in the polar lands the Eskimo would probably never have reached and passed the 80th parallel let advance rather, this was achieved solely by the food donation from the animal-rich arctic sea; seal catching was essential, who these courageous polar people across the icy sound of America to the highest north ever inhabited by humans and trained them to be such unsurpassed masters of kayaking that a skillful, persevering Eskimo the route from Rügen to Copenhagen could be covered in a day in a one-man boat. the colonization of the Hellenes, towards the tuna trains, from the Aegean Sea along the Pontic beach of Asia Minor, how that of their nautical teachers, the Phoenicians, through the Occurrence of the purple snail, which is indispensable for their dyeing, on the various shore stretches of the Mediterranean had been influenced. Where, even outside the polar world, the inland through rocky wilderness, moor and forest thicket scares people away, the sea against it a well-stocked table with fish, shellfish and crabs open, there we encounter peoples who are even almost like seabirds live exclusively on sea fare, live only on land; so extreme South end of the inhabited earth the Tierra del Fuego, in which all Scandinavian Southeast cut by fjords and torn to form coastal islands Alaska's Tlingit Indians, who are so excellent with their built slim vehicles are overgrown that they are reluctant and move clumsily on foot. With us, in Europe, it has also changed a seafaring people from the Danes who belonged predominantly to the coast formed, since a part of the same on Norway's beach below the fitting name of the Vikings, ie the settlements of the fjord people founded between a sea rich in fish and the barren Fjelden. The history of the Normans unrolls an impressive picture for us, just as bold seafarers always easily became pirates; as such the Normans soon moved their raids from their home beach to distant lands, to which the open expanse of the sea invited the brave, drove the east English rivers, the Seine, the Elbe, up the Rhine, around to burn Cologne, conquered the soil of Sicily. Same as in the deserts on the sea the saying applies that seductive is enough Prey tempts the daredevil to ambush, especially when local knowledge and a safe mountain place of the robbery promises success. The Dalmatian coast, which in the whole flank of the Adriatic ship courses one such abundance of favorable sally gates as hiding-places through her hidden rocky bays and narrow sea lanes, was, therefore, a permanent seat of piracy since ancient times; and if the Illyrian queen Teuta the emissaries of Rome at their request, to stop the robbery, proudly replied that Rome was not allowed to do that Supposing it was a custom among their people, it had a certain quality Geographic Permission. An opportunity not only makes thieves but also educates thieves. That coastal seas bays and islands fill the residents nautically suggests, has recently been somewhat overly critically questioned. Behind the smooth, insular coasts of Australia, The natives of mainland Africa have dwelt without for ages every contact with the sea. Don't say that Negroes don't show any Attachment to the seaman's profession! As some black Africans have brave sailor services rendered onboard our ships! The whole Coastal tribe of the Krunegers near Cape Palmas is world-famous even because from him the best ship hands of the West African Kauffahrtei originate, but only since these "Kruboys" in newer Time from passing ships of Europeans to such work were hired. It seems significant, however, that the Papel Negroes Portuguese West Africa south of Senegambia, this only one independent Negro people doing shipping, just there developed where the Bissagos archipelago closes to the mouth of the Rio Geba upstream. On the coast of South America, which has few islands or peninsulas the European explorers did nothing but rafting, apart from the bark barges of the Tierra del Fuego; where, on the other hand, not far from the mouth of the Orinoco the West Indian series of islands attached to the mainland, had the Caribs already had seaworthy ships that they steered with rudders and glided under cotton sails; they have feared Corsairs and had begun the conquest of the Antilles. The Westside of North America bordered again sea ignorance of the Indian tribes and increased seaworthiness together exactly where with the de Fuca Strait which enhances the fjord character of the coast. Asia like Europe shows us the main areas of their nautical development their most richly articulated exteriors. Among the Asian Seafaring peoples from Arabia to Japan are those of the most extensive tropical archipelago in the middle of this range of countries ahead of the rest insofar as we are here with the Malays have to look for the origin for excellent boat building and the starting point for the immense spread of the Malay race the countless islands of the South Seas. Since pre-Christian distances in time this gradual migration of peoples over the greatest of all oceans the same type of slender, often with outriggers against the spread, the capsizing of protected boats with the sharp keel, whose rowing power is reinforced by mat sails and the clumsy The cylindrical shape of the dugout has never appeared here. arose but there is the Polynesian variety of the light-brown race, the broadest and deepest of all branches of our race is linked to the world ocean, both materially and spiritually life up to poetry and myth; forever the balmy sea air-breathing, learning to swim earlier than walking while learning as infants already on the mother's arm through the spray of the surf, these people live a whole life on their narrow coral islands amphibious existence, almost like on firmly anchored ships in the high seas. If we look at the Indo-Arab southwest of Asia, it is revealed to us the eternal interplay of the monsoons the great promotion of shipping across the Indian Ocean; because always in the wintertime in the northern hemisphere the sailors so constantly from the monsoon to Africa east coast, then back home again in the summer months after the Indian or Arabian port, took place in this area earlier than anywhere else fertilizing intercourse between two continents and very different races across distant seas. He made the bracelets of the Indian bride from African Ivory, the expansion of Indian rice cultivation by Arabic Slave traders to the Congo, which imposed Kiswahili as Arabic Bantu negro language, which still has lively trade between German East Africa and Bombay, the permanent living of wealthy people Indian trader on our shelter coast. Finally what a shiny one A series of nautical deeds comes before our souls in the course of the ages, if we look across to Greece, Italy, the Iberian Peninsula, and the Atlantic shore countries of Western Europe! the Mediterranean navigation was awakened earlier, meanwhile, the Atlantic grew taller in antiquity, for she had to wrestle with one much more dangerous sea. With the solid Celtic ships, Venter in today's Brittany made of thick oak planks with iron Anchor chains and leather sails could be Greek or Roman Merchants don't compete. continued through the centuries Crossings of the Normans in their big rowing boats, the black ones tarred "sea rappers" from Norway to Greenland and back been more manly achievements than those, of course, the historical more consequential journey of the Columbus caravels in the calmer southern sea the compass as a guide. The great advantage of the location busiest of all oceans used, however, only in modern times for world trade and Foundation of overseas possessions the four middle-sized countries fully from France, the Netherlands, England, Germany. This most powerful boom in seafaring had to be America's first awakening goal to be unveiled to the eyes of Europe. And if yourself then also within the new world the modern greatness of shipbuilding and maritime traffic unfolded there, where endless forests were magnificent Ship lumber delivered, but especially a fine coastal structure Bays and sounds, sheltering estuary ports along with far inland into navigable streams for moderate seagoing vessels, i.e. in Canada and the Northeastern United States, so will one here as well aware of the causal link, which mostly exists between Natural endowment of the coasts and seafaring activities of the resident. However, it would be mindless pseudo-geographical fanaticism if you wanted to interpret this relationship as a natural law compulsion. The human being is not a mindless automaton; he relates to the natural stimuli of his Home sometimes like a docile, sometimes like an apathetic student. That Water from today's world port of New York once served the Indians merely for collecting edible shells; on the same archipelago that the raised Norwegians to be such bold sailors, the Lapps live on than poor fishermen. The Anglo-Saxons deepened after landing in Britain so completely in the fights with the Celts there, then in farming and animal husbandry, so that they completely turned their backs on the sea, Alfred the Great had his ships built in German shipyards had to. Most islanders in the Cyclades don't think these days of seafaring but cultivate wheat, tend the vine, or tend their goats Since the Dutch became wealthy, they neglected those of their ancestors in the harder struggle for existence so much more vigorously operated shipping, yes in the Belgian neighboring provinces The Dutchman left Brabant and Flanders to his side there as well considerable maritime traffic since ages preferably foreigners, since him on his fertile soil agriculture, trade, land trade far fed more comfortably. But does man dare to measure his strength against the elemental Dominance of the sea, he chooses as a seaman of this wrestling with storm and wave torrent even to his profession, then it applies to him fully the poet's words: "Man grows with his higher goals." The seaman's trade steels muscles and nerves, exercises sensory acuity, Presence of mind, increases with each new triumph more human Prudence over raw natural power, the courage of deliberate, fearless action. How keenly observing does the weather-beaten face peek quite habitually of our sailors under the sou'west into the distance how taciturn, however, her whole being is capable and ready for action; the apparent phlegm in the idle state corresponds to the moment of the triggering of the previous one latent cohesive force the energy and amazing endurance of performance. If the seafaring profession like in Norway or Great Britain encompasses very large sections of the population if it does so is highly respected as a cornerstone of the entire national economy and at a short distance of the coast itself from the inmost inland core has in mind all people in its pronounced peculiarity, so do not ignite the seaman's character assets even within the seafaring population by imitation. Then seize as at larger civilized nations so often, in the wake of growing familiarity with the ocean, with the earth-whole in general, maritime trade, overseas Colonization ever more extensive circles, so much of it divides the fresh enterprise, the daring, the through touch with strangers expanded intellectual horizon with the entire people. Typical of this is the contrast that lights up for us from antiquity between the brave but narrow-minded Spartan who, through his im Iron pins from overseas traffic also non-negotiable money abroad artificially fenced off between the mountain walls of its Eurotas valley conservative lived on and on the other hand the Ionian, progressive tribe of sailors, the Athenians bathed in the Aegean sea air happiest lust for action striving in the boundless expanse. Primitive man will hardly have known the ocean; later For generations, it was an object of fear and terror. as man, however, afterward dwelling permanently on its shore, its treasures exhausted, made his broad back serve to after Heart's desire to sail to the farthest coasts, so one approached him and closer, although without ever being able to put slave bonds on him. When creative deities began to be worshiped. The charming The beauty of the sea when the sailors are peaceful in the still air gliding over his mirror, out of the day's friendly the sunshine, at night the starry sky shines silver, or when the waves are whipped up in a thunderstorm, flaming lightning flashing through the gloom of sea clouds and water, -- the impact of the waves against the cliffs, the ship's battle with the storm, then the transfigured nature after the raging weather has passed, the constantly changing play of colors in a harmony of sky and water, as the country lacks in such perfection -- that has everything the poetic depiction of nature not only in Homers and Ossians Enthusiastic songs, no, even from simple impromptu songs by The primitive peoples of the beach sound natural and fresh to us, and the Painters of all seafaring nations that have risen higher in art have us in magnificent images the devotion of man in the sight of oceanic size immortalized. Knowledge and technical ability were already thereby when dealing with powerfully stimulated by the sea because of this to build the necessary vehicle and towards its ever higher perfection. And how versatile became science and technology for shipbuilding completely in Claimed since the 19th century created the steamers to cross the oceans even against wind and current! Indirectly Furthermore, the security of the ship's command has a plurality of areas of knowledge beneficially influenced. Still, life on Caroline Some old members of that strange guild, in which Exact knowledge of the position of the fixed stars about the summer and winter horizons Utilization in the boat steering inherited and at the same time such a precise Acquaintance with the location of the islands in the widest radius, like them the contemporary geography of civilized peoples were far from possessing. We thank Italian navigators for introducing the compass in our ship service due to the first recognized in China directional force of the magnetic needle. He doesn't just have countless thousands of ships, which no star shimmered in the night and fog, the shown the right way, but without the compass through all zones mass observations made by the boatmen would not have a gauss either was able to work successfully on the problem of terrestrial magnetism. and if centuries ago the Markscheider in the Klausthaler mine their subterranean passages unerringly expanded, with the pit light the Questioning the compass sounds even in this work that is truly far from the sea a fading cultural-historical echo of the tumult of the waves. However, the world sealed man to the greatest, in that it opened up the only possibility for him, the earth as a whole on the way to get to know the unveiling of the earthly face, through the World trade the economy of the individual ethnic groups to the world economy to connect, finally, through this means, all-round intercourse, like only the ocean that embraces all lands can create it, the primeval separation of the human tribes according to the individual continents to overcome, also a spiritual connection of all humanity to initiate It is understandable that world trade took the lead here himself from the not merely evil power of greed. Already calling Strabo as he saw the sailors her in the terrible dance of the waves saw life set in to transport the goods destined for Rome on the high seas before the already too shallow Tiber from the Kauffahrer to the Overloading lighter boats: "Yes, the addiction to acquisition conquers everything!" The sea has always opened the freest and, what weighs very heavily, the cheapest ways around the globe. We will soon be from the near Schantung works to deliver hard coal to Tsingtau cheaper than one of England could peddle there; on the other hand already Milan, let alone for the Italian coast is too far from us to be there on the English coast Cut out coal, because this is almost from the extraction site to Italy has the sea route ahead of our German inland coal. Oranges from Italy are sold cheaper in Hamburg than in Munich or Vienna because the sea freight from Sicily to Hamburg is not even quite as expensive as e.g. B. the land freight from Hamburg to Berlin. That's how the maritime trade throws away the cheapest freight from the most merit; around the cheap lake road not to shorten by a kilometer uselessly, they are the biggest Sea trading places in the innermost niches of sea indentations blossomed into the land; and the millions in earnings from world trade enough to deliver the vast sums that shipbuilding consumes, and to reward that guard of millions of valiant ship's crew, so that far away from their sweet home, they threatened her with constant mortal danger work, even defying the typhoons. "Barren" Homer called the sea, and yet how many goods gives them to the people, from their own, never-ending treasure, still more because they have the treasures of all the earth over theirs reflecting surface with the least imaginable impairment their marketability. About the shorelands of the sea, especially since the most intensively working temperate zones, let's look at one Reflection of which spread: the busiest cities that serve world trade as ports, shipyards, industrial sites, they want to have first-hand access to overseas-produced raw materials to bring them into Implementing art products unite with the coastal strip an abundance of smaller settlements, partly from sea trade or from coastal travel and fishing, surrounded by mostly well-stocked Fields over which the mild breeze of the sea fertilizes. The lighter the wealth to be gained is what draws people to the coast. That is why islands so often stand out against the neighboring mainland, smaller islands, other things being equal, ahead of larger ones from stronger population densification due to their relatively larger coastal portion. Where land and sea touch each other, that's where it shows naturally most evident of the sea's blessings to mankind. Finally, let's take a quick look at the meaning of the sea for the state, so it is understood from what has just been said first of all every state, if it avails itself of the advantages of the maritime affairs for its relatives, after expanding his territory to the sea, even if it were only for one to acquire such a tiny stretch of coast as Montenegro has recently been offering the Adriatic received. Because if you have one foot on the beach, you can have yours send ships around the world. What abundance of power in maritime trade, Sea supremacy, and colonization to the most remote Pontic In antiquity Miletus, in the Middle Ages Genoa, was inherited from a single town Port of unfolded! Switzerland stands for us as the only miracle building of a state in mind that, on the Alpine pinnacles in the middle of Europe founded by the vigorous industrial drive of its inhabitants to trade drifts all over the world without ever hoping for a coastal conquest to be allowed. But how embarrassingly dependent she feels about it Switzerland for the sale of goods plus goods freight from the customs facilities, the tariff rates of the railways by the four great states, which they clutch! Russia, on the other hand, offers us the greatest in world history Example of an originally purely landlocked state that purposeful advances the shores of all its surrounding seas joined, that now his banner is waving from the Baltic Sea to the Huan hai But the sea bestows three of the best, yes, on the state as such most indispensable gifts: independence, unity, and abundance of power. The sea is uninhabitable, Ratzel rightly emphasizes, thus the most secure protective wall for a state. How much less guaranteed would appear the greatest free state freedom, would have the Union to the Atlantic littoral not also conquered the Pacific! A state surrounded by the sea on all sides like that of Great Britain Japanese and now Australia, the new world island nation, can never other than point by point, namely attacked solely by the fleet attack will. France appears better due to the predominance of the maritime border covered than Germany. Because likewise the peaceful intercourse only to penetrate by ship across the coast into the interior of a state table, the state borders formed by the sea are also ethnic something more defined against the more blurred land borders ahead: they better help the unification of national ethnic mix promote and maintain. In the Roman world empire, the opposite proved to be the case only once in history the Mediterranean as those from within forced holding the mighty state together. Incessantly, however, brings the ocean of the world from the outside of all states, on the edge of which it breaks, and who understand his wake-up call, unity, and power. Greece, the Apennine peninsula lay a good one with its mountainous interior Part of their total traffic on the coastal drive, the day-to-day residents and goods from north and south, the community of interest increasing and always anew directing the gaze to the high seas beyond the home beach. Maritime trade, like any activity urgently carried out by sea, be that Large-scale industry, technical activity at sea, or colonization more than anything else to the intertwining of a nation with the wide world, but at the same time welds the inland parts of the state together firmly together with the shore, over which alone the living one Exchange between home and outside can happen, forges consequently with the hammer blows of understanding the togetherness the parts to the whole. We Germans feel that more strongly than ever in the present. No Hohenstaufe returns to the German coasts indifferently his back to lead Roman trains across the Alps; none Hanse more reluctantly strikes the flag because it is their glorious Deeds of security by Reich protection broken. a growing one Tank defense under the German Reich flag protects our merchant ships on all seas, every honest enterprise lends German ones Reich citizens in and outside of our protected areas your protective arm to the farthest beach. So flow, saved from hostile rigors, the goods of the world earned by German activity over the Threshold of the sea in all districts of our fatherland, increasing the Prosperity of our people to unprecedented heights, blessed broadening his intellectual field of vision, nourishing that of the state Makes. Our kingdom's glory is also deeply rooted in the ocean.

www.ingramcontent.com/pod-product-compliance
Lightning Source LLC
Chambersburg PA
CBHW020857160726
47993CB00004B/1705